The Children in the River

The Sequel to <u>The School Bus</u>

A Novella

Richard McCrohan

Also by the author:

The Pandora Series-

Pandora

Pandora 2

Dead to the World

Quarantine

Behold a Pale Horse

I Repeat, This is Not a Test

Other Novels-

Family Ties

Family Secrets

Family Plots

The Pittman Family Trilogy

Salvation Mountain

The School Bus

Shawtuck Asylum

What Waits Beneath

The Reunion

The Red House

Save the Last Dance for Me

Just Before Dark (a short story collection)

The Children in the River

Audiobooks-

The Pittman Family Trilogy- narrated by Skyler Morgan

Salvation Mountain- narrated by Jake Hunsbusher

The School Bus- narrated by Skyler Morgan

Shawtuck Asylum- narrated by Skyler Morgan

The Reunion- narrated by Skyler Morgan

The Red House- narrated by Duncan Storozuk

♥ For Glorya ♥

The Children in the River

Richard McCrohan

The Daily News

thedailynews.com   YOUR DAILY FAVOURITE   Oct. 16, 2020

Horrible Accident in the Oranoak River

17 Children 2 Adults Feared Dead in School Bus Crash

In *venenatis* et ut et odio. Sed ut lectus pacha. Lorem ipsum dolor sit amet, dapibus non dui. Sed posuere lectus felis. Ut facilis vehpersuetbor. Mauris neque sitem sit cras, eenvet enget accumsltar et dapos totumtem.bar erpudior et hac et facilis valor nec bus. Sed ut nunc adipiscing, kur p nal payenta. Nisi dolor Morbis ut enet. Naem vulputate dolor quis Alla. Etim, betommen adipiscing ..na. Nunc pharetra tutor a odio. sollen molestie justo. Maecenas eget dui. Nunc pellentesque aliquam magna. Suspendisse ultrices sodales dul. Vestibulum dolor dui, viverra sit. Nunc phasus tortor a odli. Vivamus et mauris hendia pharharici vn.

Continued page A2

he grevosk apprtm's sita. At vim odm lon.a castere, lutiili fuv sret pertandn. Vesfddo manandd et sed. At vim odia lo'un ortomd, lis ligcil prsec s aps steny. hus TD# PHOTO

Mercerville   Emergency Services and Police Continue to Search

SHELLY 'ON.

qu' -- p ''br q' 'thn e bt e klene! quaenus. Suscipere cui innumens singulari sien instuttunt societali argomenti. Proponere concipiam evidentia purgantur to ne verecroque ac. Corpo to nihil uollus prima et et ad. Verti est supra imo omnen sic sitas. Fomennus ubi utranique ima frigoris vim. Nia scism his illas autem vox volui tanto. Asquiri sua equidon innatis

Mercerville: January,13– State forest rangers reported finding an abandoned automobile belonging to Stephen Blurcher of Mayors Landing last night on a section of High River Road near Shawtuck State Forest. The vehicle was found idling in the road at 11:45 last night. Mr. Blurcher appears to have gotten out of his car and walked down the ravine toward the Oranoak River.

Just why he would have done that is unclear, although investigators found two other sets of smaller footprints in the same area in the ravine. A search for Mr. Blurcher was taken but called off due to snow. He remains missing.

Mercerville: March 28– Last night, traveling salesman, Robert Shapin reported seeing two young children wandering along High River Road near the state forest. Mr. Shapin stopped and called 911, but responding officers could find no trace of the children. He told the police that he could hear them as he sat and waited.

This was the fifth time police have been called to the area, since the tragic school bus accident in October and its mysterious aftermath.

Mercerville: June, 17– The Shawtuck State Forest and Nature Preserve hired professional photographer Nathan Trimble to shoot a series of pictures to be used in the new portfolio to advertise the park services. During his commission and while taking pictures of the Oranoak River, Mr. Trimble abruptly quit and walked away from his job. He refused to return nor explain why. The Mercerville Herald News was able to obtain several of the developed negatives. This was the last one taken.

Mercerville-" I often hear the sound of whispers coming out of the woods." — various Shawtuck State Forest Rangers

Mercerville- June 1: Last recorded call on police tape:
Him-"I want to report a lost child. She is wandering along
High River Road."
Her- " Bob, please don't stop. Something is terribly wrong here. Bob?"

Mercerville-October 31: The still running automobile of Mrs. Dorothy Halloran of Mayors Landing was found along High River Road yesterday morning. As of yet, she still has not been found and is considered missing.

This has been the third abandoned vehicle found in that area since the tragic school bus accident of a year ago.

A year and a half after the school bus accident...

The early morning sun shone brightly in the late July sky. Birds chirped from the trees and telephone wires. The insects had already begun their buzzing conversations. Head Park Ranger Ted Russell stood by his Dodge Ram truck and smiled as he took in the joys of a summer day in the Pennsylvania mountains. The sun felt good shining down upon his face. He paused for a second wondering if he had turned off the burner on the stove. But, Ted wondered if he had turned it off *every* morning he left the house. A couple of times he even went back, but the burner was always off. Shaking his head with a self-depreciating smile, he climbed up into the driver's seat.

Pulling out, he waved at his neighbor, Dennis Dugan, picking up his morning paper and drove off down his street. His town of Bradley was just beginning to wake up and he always enjoyed watching the world begin the new day. It wasn't long before he passed the *Welcome to Mayors Landing* sign and entered the next town. He was heading to his job in the Shawtuck State Forest Preserve at the Ranger Station and Nature Education Center. He had held the top position for ten years.

His route eventually took him past the Victoria Day Elementary School. Ted slowed down and gazed at the memorial plaque on the lawn in front. He had visited it before and knew exactly what the dedication read. It was a list of the seventeen third grade children, one teacher and their bus driver that had perished in that dreadful school bus accident a year and a half ago. An additional part was dedicated to the surviving teacher, Eleanor Hobbs, who had heroically pulled out seven of the students before the bus sank in the Oranoak River.

Ted shook his head.

That poor woman, he thought, *it must have been a nightmare dealing with the aftermath of that tragedy.* He knew that she had to seek professional psychological help dealing with the PTSD afterwards. Occasionally, when she went out, she always had a haunted look about her. Eventually Ms. Hobbs moved out of town. He had heard that she relocated to a small town in Tennessee.

He noted sadly that there were still the ubiquitous wreaths, toys, notes and flower bouquets piled in front. The citizens of Mayors Landing will never forget their lost children. Ted drove on, leaving the morbid reminders behind. The ranger now entered Mercerville and drove down Main Street. Past Palzer's Hardware, Main Street turned at the Oranoak River and became High River Road. This was the old road that ran alongside the river as it twisted and turned its way through the forest and eventually into Shawtuck State Forest. It ran through the mountains and finally into the next county at Humboldt. Fifteen years ago Route 1, a modern highway was built that avoided the forest and river and was now used almost exclusively. High River Road, or Old State Road, as it used to be called, was now only used by people visiting the State Forest or by some that were looking for a pleasant, scenic drive through the forest. Hikers and fishermen used the road to drive to their activities. But, not so much now. The Oranoak River had become the thing of urban legend. The accident, missing children, missing adults and spooky encounters had taken its toll on the adventurous nature lovers.

As he stopped at a light, he noticed an old, *Where Are Our Children*? placard in the barber shop window. At last, he turned onto High River Road and, forty-five minutes later, made a right into the gate to the State Forest Park. He got out, opened the wooden bar sealing off the entrance when it was closed, and drove inside.

Susan Cummings pinned the silver badge to her brown uniform blouse and turned towards the mirror as she straightened her clothes and squared herself away. A big smile formed on the twenty-one-year-old's face. She was pretty with a slight spray of tanned freckles across her nose and cheeks. She stood five foot six and had a slim athletic body honed by swimming and running. Her blonde hair was pulled back into a ponytail. Brightening, her blue eyes liked what they saw. Sue now stood there as a full-fledged park ranger. She had majored in land management with a minor in zoology at college and when she graduated, she wanted to enter the state government in the Park service. When a desk job at the state government bureau in Harrisburg came her way, her old tomboy ways and love of the outdoors won out over administrative work and she sought out a job as a Park Forest Ranger. She just couldn't imagine herself tied to a desk in a wallboard cubicle.

Sue entered her apartment kitchen that she had rented in Mercerville and made herself breakfast. This was her first day working at the Shawtuck State Forest Preserve. She knew that the Shawtuck Mountain Range actually started in northern New York State and ran south into Pennsylvania. People confused it with the Catskills in New York and the Poconos in Pennsylvania; but it was actually part of the Appalachian Mountains that ran across the eastern part of the country. Anyway, this was what she had read. Sue was originally from New Jersey, but went to college at Penn State.

Finishing her breakfast, she left her apartment and walked to her red Honda Civic. She had to meet her new boss Ranger Ted Russell in the park ranger office and didn't want to be late.

§   §   §

Opening the door to the ranger station, Ted threw his keys on his desk and started the coffee machine. He liked being here early. It was quiet and he found that he got a lot of work done that way. About forty-five minutes later, the door opened and Ranger Tony Wells walked in. Tony had been here for almost as long as Ted had.

"Hey, Ted," he said, "what's new?"

"Nothing Tony," Ted replied. "I got a memo that says that a high school science class from Tivoli Falls is coming in tomorrow morning."

Tony stopped and turned his head to him.

"No shit? Our first school trip since the accident," he said, surprised.

"Yeah. It's high school. I guess the lower grades are still leery."

Tony snorted. "Freakin' superstitions. I hear tell from my wife Marty that the Mercerville school board has again green lighted school trips to Shawtuck. Thank God. We can use the money."

"Better later than never," replied Ted.

Just then, Ranger Evan Smith walked in.

"Hey, guys," he said casually. Ted wasn't a stickler on rank and protocol, as long as, when it counted, they all knew who was in charge.

"Coffee up?" he inquired.

Ted looked at him sideways. "Isn't it always?"

"Every day," Evan chuckled. "Even Mondays."

"Especially Mondays," Ted laughed.

The door opened again and an unfamiliar face appeared. A blond girl walked through the door wearing a ranger uniform. She smiled awkwardly and said, "Uh...hello, I'm Susan Cummings, the new ranger hire. Uhm, Head Ranger Ted Russell?"

Ted smiled and stepped forward, extending his hand.

"That would be me, Ranger Cummings. Welcome to Shawtuck." Shaking hands with her, he introduced the others. The door opened again and Ranger Carol Baker walked inside.

Ted chuckled and said, "Last, but not least, is Ranger Carol Baker."

After introductions, everyone took a seat. Ted briefly described the duties and responsibilities of a Park Ranger for Sue's benefit.

"Today," he said in closing, "there are no tours scheduled and no groups to monitor or lead. Just the usual hikers, picnickers, family outings and nature lovers."

Everyone nodded. An easy day.

"Carol, grab one of the "Gators" and take our newbie, Sue, on a tour of the park. Familiarize her on locations and any information that she will need." Ted sighed. "Okay, gang… dismissed."

As everyone went about their business of the day, Carol came up to Sue.

"Hey, Sue, why don't you come with me and I'll give you the fifty cent tour."

"Sounds great," Sue remarked. "I'm very excited to be here."

"Think of this job as a pleasant walk in the forest that you actually get paid to take," Carol said.

"Really?"

"No, not really," Carol chuckled. "Babysitting some of the people that come up here can be a chore. You won't believe some of the families that we sometimes get. Ha! *Sure, Timmy, it's okay to play with the* bears☐shooting *birds with your slingshot is okay, this is a forest and you're* hunting☐oh, *oh, the barbecue is on fire.* We get them all. But otherwise, yeah, it's great being here with nature."

Sue was laughing.

"I can only imagine," she said.

"No, you couldn't," Carol said with a laugh. "The end of last year, a couple of teens snuck off to screw in the woods. They wound up lying in a bunch of poison ivy. Got a rash everywhere. And I mean everywhere. They tried to sue the state, saying that the patch wasn't properly marked. I swear to God. Morons."

By now, Sue was hysterical.

"Oh, my God, that's priceless."

With a smirk, Carol said, "Yeah, it was. Although the couple was really itching to be paid." Again, Sue was laughing uproariously.

The two women climbed aboard one of the three Gators in the lot. A Gator was an all-terrain vehicle made by John Deere called the Gator and used to carry supplies and travel through the large forest.

§   §   §

Two hours later, a silver Lexus SUV pulled into the park's parking lot. Todd Nyland got out followed by his family: Kelly, his wife, Becky, their eight-year-old daughter and Jason and Jessie, their five-year-old twins. Todd and his family had come from Scranton to have a little nature outing and a picnic in the state park before returning home.

Kelly and Todd changed shoes and looked around the area. The pungent smell of pine pervaded the parking lot and beyond. Smiling, Todd remembered his youth in summer camp. Hiking, swimming, canoeing and playing sports were his whole summer and he loved it. He wanted his children to experience nature like he did. They couldn't afford the camps that he wanted to send them to, but next year he would be able to. This was their second prize. Complete with their hiking shoes, the Nyland family marched into the park ranger building to get familiar with the park and start their outdoor adventure.

§ § §

Ted Russell got a call from Evan telling him that Frank Riesling had just pulled up across from the old crash site. Hanging up the phone, he closed his eyes and thought, *Oh, shit.*

Ever since his two children had perished in the school bus accident a year and a half ago, and then his wife apparently committed suicide at the site later on, the poor man had been an absolute basket case. Ted had found her car that day parked across from the smashed wooden guardrail, and fearing the worst when he didn't see her, climbed down the embankment to see if she was somehow there. All he found was a woman's shoe at the end of the rocky shore into the river. Her body was later found by a man walking his dog miles down the river. At her funeral (two weeks after his own children's) he was inconsolable. Ted later learned that he took a leave of absence from work and began drinking heavily. Now, every so often, he would drive up to the infamous site and sit on the newly repaired guardrail with a bottle. Concerned for his health and safety whenever he found out that he was here, Ted would go down and sit with them until he could convince him to go home. Ted hated this responsibility. But, he thought it was his duty to do so. It was torture to his soul. When he looked into the eyes of a man who had lost virtually everything meaningful in his life, he did not like what he saw there.

Ted reluctantly got into a Gator and drove down to the entrance of the park and turned left. About a quarter of a mile down, he saw Frank's car parked off on the far shoulder. He made a U-turn and pulled up behind him. Frank was not sitting in his usual position on the guardrail.

Alarmed, Ted got out and trotted over to the edge of the embankment. He looked around and then called out his name. Hearing nothing, Ted stepped over the guardrail and carefully climbed down the steep embankment to the river. Most of the destroyed foliage from the crash had by now grown back. Nature always prevails no matter what. As he worked his way down, he saw Frank Riesling standing on one of the large flat rocks along and into the river. The scars from the tumbling bus were still evident etched on to the surface of the stones.

"Frank," Ted called out as he reached the bottom. "What are you doing down here? You usually stay up on the guardrail. What's up?"

Frank turned his head slightly at the sound of Ted's voice. Then he turned back to the river. As Ted came up to him, he placed his hand on his shoulder. Frank stiffened. After a second, he turned to the ranger.

"She's here. I know she is. She's here."

Ted looked out into the gurgling river. The current here in this part of the waterway was still very strong and he could see the small whitecaps of the warring currents. But nothing else.

"Who's here, Frank?" Ted asked. He already knew the answer.

"Sam," Frank said with a vacant smile. "My daughter. She's still here."

"Yes, I know, Frank," Ted said slowly. "Samantha is still here. They never found her body."

Frank turned his head to Ted and then quickly turned back to the river. He seemed to be looking for something.

"No, you don't understand," Frank said oddly, "she's here. *Really* here. My Sam. I hear her. She's calling to me."

A sheet of goose-bumps rose on Ted's arms. He looked at the river.

"Frank," Ted said strongly, "Sam is not here. She's not here, and I'm very sorry, but she is not alive. It's been a year and a half. She's gone, Frank. Your daughter is gone. I'm sorry."

Frank turned to him uncertainly. He seemed confused.

"But, you didn't hear her?" he asked, almost pleadingly.

"No, Frank," Ted replied. "I didn't hear a thing. Just the river, that's all." He gently guided the distraught man away. "Come on, Frank, let's go back up to the road."

He steered the reluctant man up the hill, slipping once or twice. When they returned to High River Road, Ted took him to his car.

"Go home, Frank. Get some help. This isn't doing you any good. Please. See someone."

Mumbling, Frank sat down in the seat and after a minute or two, started up his vehicle. He looked back up at Ted with tears in his eyes.

"You…you really didn't hear her?"

"No, Frank," Ted answered. "There was no one there." He patted him on the back.

Putting the car into drive, Frank paused, then turned the car around and drove back home.

Ted watched him go sadly. He sat down on the guardrail and let out a deep breath. He was emotionally exhausted.

After a minute, he stood up and started for his vehicle. He abruptly stopped, listening carefully; Ted looked toward the river and then quickly ran to the Gator and started it up. With a screech of gravel, he drove away as fast as possible.

God help me, he thought as he shook, *I did hear something.*

§   §   §

Completing the tour, Carol turned the Gator around and the two women started back.

"So that's about it," Carol said. "Pretty straightforward."

"Great," Sue replied, smiling. "Nothing else I should know?"

There was a very pregnant pause. Sue turned to the other woman.

"So…nothing else?"

Carol grinned, embarrassed and said, "Well, there was that bus accident almost two years ago."

"What do you mean?" Sue asked.

"About a year and a half ago, a school bus from Mayors Landing, two towns away, crashed through the guardrail right down the road and plunged into the Oranoak River. They were supposed to be coming here for a third grade field trip."

"Oh, my God," Sue exclaimed, turning in her seat, "that's terrible. Was anyone hurt?"

Carol glanced at her. "Nineteen people in total were killed. Seventeen children and two adults."

Sue was aghast. She had no idea.

"Jesus, what happened?"

Carol shrugged her shoulders. "I don't really know. They say the bus driver had a massive heart attack and accidently drove the bus off the road and down into the river. It was a horror show. The Mercerville police actually found the bus after a big search."

"That is terrible," said Sue shaking her head. She had tears in her eyes.

"Yeah," said Carol simply.

"But that was a year and a half ago, right?" Sue asked.

"Yes."

Sue continued to stare at Carol until she couldn't take it anymore and pulled over. She looked at Sue and said, "But, that's not all."

Carol grimaced and fidgeted in her seat until Sue asked quietly, "What else?"

Looking at her uncomfortably, Carol continued, "When they found the bus a few miles downriver and pulled it out... there were still five missing children that weren't accounted for. They figured that they were taken by the strong river currents and were lost miles upstream."

Sue grimaced at the news, but continued to look at Carol. She had a feeling that this wasn't the end.

Carol leaned over and spoke as if she were telling the world's biggest secret.

"About a week or two after, the mother of two of the dead kids went up to the site. She apparently committed suicide there by drowning herself. And a while after that seven more kids were found missing while visiting the site."

"What… seven kids?" Sue exclaimed.

"Yeah, they found their bikes parked on the grass along the road."

"What happened to them?" Sue asked.

"Nobody knows. They just disappeared. The police figured they fell into the river."

"What, all seven of them?"

"Hey, nobody knows."

Sue was flummoxed.

"Not only that, but there have been other missing people and some claiming to have seen things on High River Road at night."

Sue looked at her askance. "Wait... you're just messing with me, right?"

"No, I swear to God. Don't tell Ted that I told you this. He really doesn't like to talk about this. Ever."

§ § §

As the day progressed, everything was running well at the park. Carol and Sue had finished their tour. Evan was on the lookout for a black bear that had been spotted by some hikers. Ted and Tony were traveling around the park checking on things. All was well.

§ § §

The Nyland family had hiked around the trails. Todd and Kelly were taking turns pointing out all of the flora and fauna in the forest. Both parents were educators and were able to hold their children's fascination for all that time. Even the twins.

Now it was lunchtime and both parents had planned a wonderful picnic lunch for the family. Hot dogs, hamburgers and a lot of healthy salads. The barbeques were near the ranger station just up from the entrance. The area was surrounded by woods, so as to give the aura that the families were indeed camping.

Eight year old Becky had to pee, so Kelly took her up to the bathrooms near the ranger station. Jason and Jessie were down at the picnic table eating potato chips.

Todd was having a bit of trouble getting the grill to light; and then to get the flames up to level. He was very frustrated. It was now one-thirty.

Kelly and Becky came down from the rest area and Kelly told Becky to go down to the picnic table with the twins. As she walked up to Todd, he had finally gotten the fire going and was just now putting on the franks and burgers.

"How's it going, Chef?" Kelly asked.

"Finally got the knack of it," Todd said, proudly.

Kelly turned to look off to the table. She saw only Becky sitting there eating potato chips.

"Where are the twins?" she asked.

Todd turned to her. "Huh? They're at the table."

"No, they're not," Kelly said, worried.

Todd looked over and his jaw dropped. Kelly ran down and called to Becky.

"Where are Jason and Jessie?"

With a mouthful of chips, Becky shrugged and said, "I don't know."

Immediately, the fire forgotten, Todd and Kelly ran around calling the twins' names.

"Jessie! Jason! Where are you?"

As they ran around the picnic area yelling, Tony came up to them, asking what was wrong.

Soon the three of them were running around asking anyone if they saw them.

"Hey," Tony called over to a young couple exiting their car. "Have you seen a little boy and girl wandering around?"

"Not really," the young man noted, "but I did see three little kids walking down to the entrance gate."

"When?" Tony asked, excitedly.

"A couple of minutes ago, I guess," he replied.

Tony ran down the paved drive as fast as he could. The only thing past the gate was the road and then the river.

As he came into view of the roadway, he saw three little kids on the other side of the guardrail start down the embankment to the river.

Reaching the street, Tony started to call their names when he stopped short, almost being hit by a car coming by. Almost falling back on his ass, he once again darted across the road. Vaulting the guardrail, he ran pell-mell down the embankment, slipping dangerously, but miraculously not falling. There on the rocky shoreline stood two little children, a boy and a girl.

"Hey, kids," Tony shouted, "wait. Be careful."

They turned and looked at him, not at all scared or frightened. As he reached them, Tony said, "Where is the other kid? Where is your friend?"

The two children looked around, puzzled.

"I don't know," the girl said. "Jeffrey was right here. I don't see him now."

The boy looked at his sister, now a little bit frightened. "Where did Jeffrey go, Jessie?"

Puffing hard, Tony went down on one knee facing the little girl. "Who is Jeffrey?" he asked her.

"He was our new friend," she responded. "He wanted us to come down here and meet his other friends. He said that they were waiting for us."

"Where did you meet Jeffrey?" Tony asked, now afraid.

"He was in the woods," Jessie said.

"And he was waiting for us," Jason added.

§   §   §

After a reunion with their parents, Tony managed to finesse his way out of the question of who was Jeffrey. Ted arrived at this point and Tony pulled him aside. He explained the entire incident. The Nyland family, tearful and relieved, headed back toward their now well burnt picnic lunch, grateful to the rangers and happy to be together again.

Ted guided the very upset and agitated Tony back toward the station.

"Do you know who Jeffrey was?" Tony said through gritted teeth. Ted looked at him helplessly.

"He was Jeffrey Williams. One of those fucking kids that went missing from that fucking bus accident. You know it and I know it. Christ!" Tony turned away.

Then he quickly spun back to Ted.

"When the hell does this shit end? When? I feel like I'm living in some kind of fucked up horror movie."

"I know," was all Ted could say.

"You know?" Tony said, raising his voice. Ted spun him around and walked them away.

"Everybody fucking knows!" Tony continued. "This is a nightmare that just doesn't stop. What are we going to do about this? Shit. This can't go on. It just can't. I'm thinking of turning in my papers and just quitting the whole fucking thing. Really."

"Let's... let's just let it ride for now," Ted replied. "Let's see what happens. This has to end sometime."

§   §   §

For the next month everything went normally.

§   §   §

At eleven o'clock in the morning, Frank Riesling, after an evening of drinking until he passed out on the couch, got up and went to his car in the garage. He was determined to find out if his daughter was still alive. She must be. He had heard her. She called to him. He had most definitely heard her speak to him. She wanted them together. They must be together. His wife, his son, his daughter□gone. Now it was only him. He was alone. In a blurry instance of semi-clarity, he surmised that, yes, they should be together. But as they were dead, they were not coming back to him. As the absolutely inconsolable man sat there, he realized then that he must go to them. Frank started his car. Then, he closed the garage doors and opened up all of the windows in his car.

"Don't worry, Sam. And Isaac, and Carol. I'm coming to you now. I'll see you all soon."

Then he closed his eyes and waited.

§   §   §

It was now the beginning of October. The weather was unusually warm for this time of year. Some thought it was from Global Warming, while the old-timers figured it was just Mother Nature. Never-the-less, all were thankful for a few more weeks of good weather. There were no further incidents along the Oranoak River. Ted had noticed Lily Freeman putting up a new memorial wreath for her son Jimmy, who had gone missing along with four of his friends in the river exactly two years ago. The authorities found their bicycles at the accident site, along with the bikes of two other older boys. No one knew what had happened to the seven of them. The police had termed it "death by misadventure." Drowning was naturally assumed.

After all, the currents there in the river were deceptively strong and even standing in the waters there could carry a young boy away fairly quickly. They did find a Philadelphia Phillies baseball cap along the shoreline floating in a pool that was determined to belong to Rickie Carlton. His father said that he loved that hat and would never have left it intentionally.

Ted had heard through the grapevine that a company in Suskill on the other side of the Shawtuck Forest Preserve was seeking to get permission to build a large marina at the Oranoak River's edge. The Oranoak, after it flowed through the Shawtuck Mountains widened at the first town past that, which was Amberton. The river then lost the swift currents that had categorized it from its origins, and became wider and more placid. The Oranoak eventually merged into the Suskill River and from there into the Susquehanna River.

The city of Suskill wanted to have a large marina for boats (both pleasure and fishing) to dock at their shores.

A resort type of atmosphere was what they were looking for. Their permit was now tied up in local politics (read bribes and promises). But soon that was expected to clear once the, *ahem,* amounts were agreed upon.

§   §   §

Sue Cummings was sitting at the counter in Millie's Diner, the local "meet and greet" eatery on Main Street in Mercerville. She was having a BLT on rye toast and a cup of coffee. Today's paper was folded in front of her. As she perused the paper, she saw that Paltzer's Hardware Store was having a fall sale. Sue knew that she should probably get a new winter scraper and brush for her car. The old one was in bad shape and she should use this opportunity to replace it. Below the ad was a notice that the Holy Mother Catholic Church was going to be holding a two year memorial service for Michael LoPresti and Andrew Kozak, two of Mercerville's children who had presumably drowned in the Oranoak River. They were still missing.

The local assumption was that the five smaller boys, Jimmy, Davey, Kenny, Rickie and Gary must have fallen into the river somehow and the two older boys tried to save them. No one knew for sure, but that scenario suited the town of Mercerville just fine. Anything else was absolutely unthinkable.

Just then she felt somebody sit down in the seat next to her. Looking over, she saw a young police officer sitting beside her. He took off his uniform hat and put it down. Looking over, he smiled at her warmly.

"Hi. I've seen you around town. You're new here, aren't you?" he asked.

"Yes, I am. Only three months here, officer," she said coquettishly, with a returned smile.

He chuckled. "Please," he said, "you can call me Pat. Pat Kaiser. I'm relatively new on the squad, too. Only a year and a half."

"And I'm Sue Cummings. Nice meeting you."

The waitress came over and the cop ordered a coffee and a roll with butter.

"What do you do, Sue? Do you work around here?"

"I'm a park ranger in the Shawtuck Forest Preserve," she replied.

"Really!" Pat exclaimed. "That's neat. I love the outdoors myself. How did you become a park ranger?"

Sue explained, "I majored in land management and minored in zoology in college. Since I, too, love the outdoors, I decided to be a ranger. I love the job. It's right up my alley." She was looking at the young cop as she spoke. He was tall, with light brown hair and a mustache. Pat had a youthful face and Sue assumed that he had the facial hair to make himself look older and more mature. He was well built, too. *Not too bad,* she thought.

Pat said, "I went to a two year college, but had no idea what I wanted to do, so I dropped out. My dad had a friend on the force and he spoke with me. It sounded good...good pension, good benefits, so I thought, "What the hell," and joined. It's interesting work; I like it. Always something different."

The two talked for a while, until Pat had to go back on patrol.

"So, Sue, do you think you'd like to go out with me sometime?"

Smiling, she answered, "Sure. I'd love to, Pat. How about this Saturday?"

"Perfect. I'm off duty. We can catch a movie in the Route 1 Lowe's Multiplex."

They exchanged numbers.

He got up off of the stool, said good-bye, then, dropping some money on the check, grabbed his hat and left.

The waitress came over.

"Will you be having dessert?" she said with a smirk and a wink.

Laughing out loud, Sue said, "Ha, how about a piece of your cherry pie I've been hearing so much about?"

"Coming right up."

Sue sat thinking as she waited for her pie. She thought it was a little bit weird that when people in town heard she was a park ranger, they seemed to get a bit uneasy. One thing she found out pretty fast was that Shawtuck and the Oranoak River were not subjects you wanted to bring up in casual conversation around Mercerville and Mayors Landing. It almost seemed to be like the villagers and Frankenstein's Castle. Everyone knew that something strange was going on, but nobody wanted to talk about it.

She remembered about a month ago, she stopped for gas at the Mobil station down on Brookside and the kid working the pumps saw her uniform. He kept asking her if she ever saw any of the kids from the bus. She told him he watched too much TV, but he was insistent. He said that the "Murder Bus" used to be stored in the back lot. She had gotten real annoyed and told him just to fill up her tank and cut the gab. Afterwards, she switched to using the Seven-Eleven gas pumps a couple of blocks away. Too weird.

§   §   §

Ted Russell was doing some paperwork at his desk. The state was always requiring some study or another. Most of the work was bullshit and truthfully, didn't make much sense or was about some small matter that was really of no consequence. Busy work.

The door opened and Tony Wells came inside.

"Hey, Ted," he said, "I took another look for that bear that some of the hikers said they saw. I couldn't find any sign of him. I even looked for any scat, but didn't see any around. I guess he's gone."

Ted looked up at him. "He was probably looking for an easy source of food to fatten up before hibernation."

"Seems so," Tony remarked. He sat down in the chair in front of the desk.

Ted leaned back in his chair.

"We have a class field trip coming in tomorrow from Bradley Elementary School. Fifth graders. They want to see the autumn leaves and take the Changing Colors Tour. Thank God."

Tony only nodded his head. He had his elbows on the arms of the chair and his fingers tented under his nose.

"Something bothering you, Tony?"

The ranger sat there for a second. Ted waited patiently. Tony raised his eyes to Ted and then lowered them to some vague point on his desk.

"You know that fisherman we had yesterday that broke his leg fishing in the river?"

"Oh, yeah, that old guy," Ted nodded. "Bob something or other. Wait, Zimmerman, Bob Zimmerman. From one of those towns north of Shawtuck. He was trying to wade out and lost his footing. The old guy slipped and broke his leg. Luckily, he wasn't too deep and was able to hobble back in before he called us."

"You sent Carol and me down to help him," Tony noted.

"I did," Ted said, unsure of where this was going.

Tony took a deep breath and blew it out. "We called the EMS and as we were helping him up the embankment, do you know what he said to me?"

Folding his hands in front of him on the desk, Ted asked, "No, what did he say?"

"He asked me if we had a class of school kids up in the park and were giving a tour."

Ted scrunched his eyes in puzzlement. "Why?"

"He told me that while he was fishing, he could hear the sound of children laughing. That was right before he slipped." Ted opened his mouth to speak, but Tony interrupted.

"I went back after we got him up on the road because he had dropped his pole and asked if I could get it for him because it was expensive. I saw it caught on a rock near where he fell and as I reached for it, do you know what I saw? I saw a piece of that yellow school bus in the water. That is what he must have slipped on."

"Well, that's an eerie coincidence. I know that there are still pieces of that bus scattered around in the water," Ted remarked.

Now looking directly into his eyes, Tony continued, "And that wasn't the worst. As I was walking to shore, I thought I could hear that laughter, too."

"Tony," Ted sighed, "I think your imagination is getting to you."

"No, Ted, I really don't think that it is," he replied. "Just like I know it wasn't my imagination that I saw three kids climbing over the guardrail." He paused. "You know me Ted. I've been here almost as long as you have. You know I'm not a superstitious kind of guy. You and I have been denying that something very strange has been going on around here ever since that school bus crashed through the guardrail and went into the Oranoak River. And...and those five little kids they never found? I don't know... something happened in that damned river. The teacher that survived, she was never the same. Those children that were rescued…they heard things. Then, all those other kids that went missing? Something's not right."

"I□" Ted started.

"And then we have all these people that have called in sightings of seeing kids on the road. That one car last winter where the driver went down to the river in the snow… what the hell happened to him?"

Ted looked down at his hands.

"I don't know, Tony," he said softly. "I don't know what happened to him. I don't know where the missing children are and I don't know about that photographer's photo, either. The voices…nothing. I just don't fucking know. But, I really, really don't think that there are ghosts, or that the river is haunted or anything. And why? Because I don't want to believe it. I can't believe it. Because if I did, then I think my head would explode."

Tony sat there looking defeated. After several minutes of silence, he said in a near whisper, "I don't know what I'm going to do."

"Tony," Ted said, "you have a ton of vacation time coming to you that you've accumulated. Why don't you take some of that time and you and Marty take a little vacation. Maybe Florida or some place with a beach. I think it would probably be good for the both of you."

Tony sighed and rubbed his eyes with the heels of his palms.

"Yeah, maybe you're right, Ted. I think this is all getting to me. Maybe I'm going loony. I don't know. Thanks Ted. I think I'll take you up on your suggestion." He smiled sadly and got up. As he walked to the door, he turned to Ted and nodded, then walked out of the room.

§   §   §

That night Sue and Pat were seated at a corner table in Vesuvio's Restaurante in Mayors Landing. It was the best Italian restaurant in the area. Pat poured them more wine.

"That's a nice wine, Pat," Sue told him.

"This is my favorite Barolo," he replied proudly.

This was their fourth date. They had just finished their entrées and were sitting over the remnants of the bottle.

"So, back to the story. What happened after you pulled up?" she asked

Pat laughed, "I pulled up in front of the house and a lady runs out the front door. She had called in a domestic disturbance, so I don't know exactly what to expect. She looked terrified and I asked her what happened. Ha, ha. So, she pointed up to a tree in her front yard and says, "My kitty climbed up the tree and won't come down." I looked at her as if she was nuts. You said it was a domestic disturbance, I said. It is, she tells me. Can you get him down for me? I looked up in the tree at this tabby cat and then I say to her, yeah, I think so. I'm a pretty good shot."

Sue begins laughing hysterically.

"She looks at me," Pat continued, "and then passes out right there on the lawn." Now they're both laughing.

"No…" Sue says.

"I swear," Pat said, holding his hand up.

"Did you get into trouble?"

"Nah, not really. This lady had a habit of calling the police for any little bit of nonsense, so my Sergeant just told me to keep the humor down. Of course, he was laughing, too."

"That is just too funny," she said, taking another sip of wine.

"How about you, Sue?" Pat asked. "What was the funniest thing that ever happened to you on the job?"

"Oh," she said with a huge grin, "I don't even have to think about that one. Two weeks into my job, these two young people drive into the park. They're furries."

"They're what?" Pat asked.

"Furries. You know, people who think they are animals and dress-up in animal costumes?" Sue answered.

"Really?" laughed Pat.

"I swear to God. They are all over. Even in the schools," she said. Pat shook his head in disbelief.

"So anyway, these two get out of their car and they are dressed up like chipmunks. They go traipsing off into the woods. I'm watching them, you know, because... well... they are just so weird. Now the trees are full of real squirrels running around and Chip and Dale run up like they're relatives." Pat is now guffawing. "The girl, as I found out later, starts to climb up the tree to be one with the squirrels, and as she is climbing, the squirrels attack her. She was only as high as the first branch, and slipped off. The back of her costume gets caught on the branch and she's swinging there, screaming her head off, while he is standing beneath her and reaching up and trying to pull her down. Her costume rips in two and she lands on top of him. The bottom half of her suit is still up in the tree and she has no clothes on underneath."

They are laughing so hard that tears are running from their eyes.

"She gets up, still screaming, and starts running back to their car… the top half of her, a chipmunk, and the bottom half, a naked girl. He, still in costume, is running after her. Everybody around just stood there applauding."

Still laughing, Pat emptied the bottle into their glasses and replied, "Well, that one beats mine by a mile." He took out his wallet and put a credit card on top of the check.

"After we finish the wine," Sue said, looking at him through lidded eyes, "why don't we go to my place?"

Smiling, Pat said, "That's the best thing I've heard all day."

Simultaneously, they both had the same thought□ *this is going to be a great evening.*

§   §   §

Ted had put a burger on the grill in his backyard. His wife had left him five years ago. He loved the outdoors and forests and she loved big cities and high-rises. They tried to make it work, but they were just too far apart on that and apparently almost everything else. They were now apart, but they were both happier.

Taking another pull on his bottle of beer as he flipped the patty, he thought of his conversation with Tony Wells.

He remembered back to the day that the school bus accident had occurred. That part of the river was considered to be part of state land and he had to be there as mandated. When he heard the call that they found the survivors he had gone down and helped the two officers bring the children and teacher up onto the side of the road. He had brought several blankets to wrap around the wet and cold children. Ted kept them together as the two cops rescued everyone. Ted would never forget a couple of the drenched children that asked him and their teacher, "What about our friends out there? Are they coming, too? We heard them." The look that Eleanor Hobbs had given him at that moment froze him to the bone. There was a look in her eyes that he had never seen before nor since. That was something he had never told anyone. At the time he did not understand exactly what was happening and what they actually meant. He did now. One of those poor kids that he held had actually died in his arms as the EMS vans pulled up. He never told anyone about that either. He had cried himself to sleep that night.

Ted was pretty pragmatic. He never put much credence in the supernatural. Sure, as a boy, he loved watching scary monster movies. Hell, what boy didn't love that kind of thing. But as he grew older and realized that the horror movies were just Hollywood imagination, he never believed the tropes. He didn't believe in ghosts. He always figured that when you're dead, you're dead. Period. No more real than vampires, or other such nonsense. But since the school bus accident, his core beliefs had been shaken. It's not that he actually thought the school bus or the river were haunted because, truthfully, he just didn't think that kind of stuff happened. But Ted had to admit to himself that something very, very wrong was at work here. Tony was even more prone to hard realism then he was. The fact that he said that he saw a third child at the river and even heard their laughter was nothing to take lightly. Tony would absolutely never even admit to that unless he was very troubled. Ted never saw anything amiss, and, except for that one time with Frank Riesling, heard anything like Tony or the surviving school kids heard. But that didn't mean anything. He trusted the experiences that he had been told of. There were just too many of them to write off as figments of imagination. He was confused not only in what was happening, but also in what to do about it all.

Tomorrow was the Bradley school field trip and he intended to supervise it along with Sue. He was a little bit worried about it, which was why he wanted to be there. He had picked Sue to be with him because she was new and didn't have those experiences to color her views.

After fixing his burger, getting another beer and eating, he still didn't know what to make of the whole thing.

And an inner voice told him☐ it wasn't over.

§   §.   §

The fifth graders stepped down from their bus looking around the park preserve. Some of the boys began to roughhouse until their teachers intervened.

Ted and Sue walked over to the group. One of the teachers, a thin man in his fifties with eyeglasses and a closely trimmed beard that was beginning to get gray, stepped up to them.

"Hello, Rangers. I am Carl Tauber one of the Bradley Elementary School #3 teachers. My comrade here is Ms. Gwen Peevers, the other fifth grade teacher."

"I am Park Ranger Ted Russell and this is Ranger Sue Cummings." They shook hands. "We will be your guides for this trip. I understand that the changing colors of the fall season is to be your focus on this trip?"

"Yes," Carl nodded, "we'd like to teach the kids the how and why of what happens. This way they can see it and understand it for themselves."

The other teacher smiled and said, "What better place than a huge forest, right?"

"Sounds good," Ted laughed. "Let's get started." He and Sue introduced themselves to the boys and girls in front of them. There were eighteen in all.

"Okay, gang," Ted started off, "who can tell me why the leaves are all these beautiful colors today?"

Several hands rose (mostly the girls).

"Photosynthesis," one girl called out.

"Ooo, 'fraid not, young lady," Ted chuckled good-naturedly. "Not exactly. But a good guess. Photosynthesis is the word for how the plants convert water and carbon dioxide into carbohydrates with the help of the sun. It's how they live. Anyone else?" Three more hands quickly dropped. Ted gestured to Sue.

She smiled and cleared her throat. "When photosynthesis works in plants it makes chlorophyll which also makes plants green. As autumn comes and the daylight grows shorter and it gets colder, that chlorophyll breaks down and begins to lose its color. That's when we start to see yellow, orange and red start to appear."

"The green changes color?" one boy asked.

"No, the green chlorophyll disappears. The other colors were always there, but the green covered them up and hid them."

"Cool," another boy said. "Can I take a green leaf and scrape the green off with my fingernail?"

Ted laughed aloud. "Wow, nice going. That was the first time I was ever asked that question. Good one." The boy beamed and high-fived his friends. "No, I'm afraid you can't."

"But after they turn brown they die, right?" a girl said sadly.

"That's true," Ted agreed. "The tree actually lets that happened to save itself during the winter. Leaves need a lot of water which evaporates into the air. That takes away from the roots getting enough water. This way the roots will get enough water to live through the winter and next year it will make new leaves."

The children murmured amongst themselves, digesting this news.

"Man," another boy complained, "science is really complicated. How do you know all this stuff?"

"By going to school and studying hard," Sue said quickly. This time, the teachers beamed. "You could all know this too, and a whole lot more. All you have to do is stay in school, study hard and learn things. It's as easy as that."

From the back of the group, a girl said, "Yeah, but studying is really hard."

Sue piped up and said, "If studying wasn't hard, then everybody would know this stuff. But if you know all that and others don't, then I guess that makes you pretty special." The two teachers were smiling and looking at each other as they saw the group gnawing their lips in thought and nodding.

"Hey," Ted said, laughing, "it's a good thing that that only happens to trees and not humans. Imagine your hair turning different colors and then falling out in the winter."

The children laughed hysterically, pointing at one another and saying, "You'd be bald!" The two teachers were delighted with the way the trip was going.

"Come on, everyone. Let's all go into the forest as a group and look at all the different leaves and colors. See if we can find which type of leaves have the most awesome colors."

"Yay," they all yelled.

§   §   §

Two hours later, the group was way up the trail looking around at the multi-colored leaves and pointing out any bird or animal that they saw. The two rangers were sure to name any fauna that the kids saw. And they saw a lot. They would add a little bit of scientific knowledge to the explanations. Everything was going beautifully.

Ted was having a good time. He actually really enjoyed these school field trips. His wife didn't want to have children and, as much as he did, he acquiesced to her wishes. These trips filled the lonely spots for him.

Happening to glance over at Sue as she pointed out something to a small group of girls, he suddenly saw her pick her head up and look around quizzically. Her brows were furrowed. Ted walked over and asked,

"Everything okay, Sue?"

She looked around puzzled.

"Uh…yeah…yeah, Ted."

She glanced at the girls and asked, "Wasn't the woman teacher named Peeves? Gwen Peeves?"

"Yes, why?" Ted asked.

"I don't know," Sue said unsurely. "I could have sworn I heard one of the girls say, "I don't want to see any spiders, Mrs. Hobbs."

"You must have misheard," Ted shrugged.

He turned and started to walk away, when he stopped short. *Mrs. Hobbs. That was the name of the teacher who saved some of the children in the accident. Mrs. Hobbs.* He observed the girls and then gazed into the woods. He saw nothing. A cold chill ran up his spine.

Looking at Sue again, talking animatedly and laughing with the children, Ted could see that the name meant nothing to her. Thank God.

§   §   §

At last it was time to start heading back to the bus. There were sandwiches and juice boxes waiting for the kids. Carl came up to Ted as they walked back.

"Terrific day, Ranger Ted. Thank you so much. This was great fun and a good teaching lesson for our classes."

"I'm glad that you enjoyed it, Mr. Tauber. It *was* fun. Nature is always wonderful to be around and to engage with."

Out of the corner of his eye, he could see three boys walking off to the side. They were whispering to each other and seemed to be nudging the third boy over to Ted as they walked. He was reluctant, and kept whispering "No," to the other two.

He looked at the teacher and saw that he noticed it also.

Smiling amusedly, Ted asked, "Is there a question you boys have for me? Something we haven't covered?"

With a final nudge, the boy was now next to Ted, walking. He seemed embarrassed.

"Well…my friends, uhm…"

"You want to ask me something? It's okay. Ask away."

"Okay," the boy said, getting up his nerve. He glanced sideways ay his two friends and Ted could hear them whispering, "Go ahead, ask him."

Ted was trying his best not to laugh.

"Uhm, yeah. Well…" he glanced again at his friends. Then boldly, he turned to Ted and said abruptly,

"What about the dead kids? Where are they? We didn't see any."

Ted's bemused smile disappeared. The teacher pinched his lips together in annoyance and humiliation.

"Dead kids?" Ted asked neutrally. "There aren't any dead kids in the park. Why would there be?"

Although his friends did and immediately backed off, the boy hadn't noticed his teacher's malevolent glare.

"We heard that those kids in the bus accident are around the river and the woods and stuff. I even heard my mom say☐"

Ted cut him off.

"Well, I'm happy to tell you that there are no dead kids anywhere near here. Anything that you might have heard are just silly stories."

"Bruce…" Carl warned between his gritted teeth.

Ted turned to him with a smile and winked at him to relieve the tension. Turning back to Bruce (who himself looked like he wanted to die) Ted grinned and said to him,

"Besides, Bruce, we don't allow dead kids into the park. Against the rules, you know."

Bruce's mouth dropped open.

"What? Really?"

Ted started chuckling uncontrollably, and before long, he, Bruce, Carl and the other two boys were laughing and joking.

After the classes were getting back on the bus to depart, Carl came up to Ted and shook his hand.

"I'm sorry about Bruce. That was□"

"Don't worry about it. It was nothing. Urban legends. What are you going to do?"

Finally, the bus pulled away.

Sue came up to him.

"What was that all about?"

Ted waved his hand, dismissively, "Ah, nothing. Just a goofy kid."

"Oh, good," she said in relief. "I think the field trip went splendidly. I'll go up and start the paperwork, boss."

Ted nodded, as Sue walked off.

Ted turned and stared off into the park in the afternoon's waning light. His face tightened as he stood there.

I don't want to see any spiders, Mrs. Hobbs.

Again, he shivered.

§   §   §

Pat and Sue were sitting at the dining room table in his house, each sipping on a bottle of beer. A slew of open and empty cardboard cartons of Chinese take-out were scattered along the wooden table.

Putting her beer down, Sue sighed heavily and said, "Oh, my God, I don't think I ate that much in my entire life. I'm going to explode."

Tilting his head back and finishing his beer, he placed the bottle on the table noisily across from her.

"I'm done," he pronounced in finality. "I can't eat another drop."

Sue looked over the cartons and dirty plates on the table and asked, "Do we have to move now? I seriously don't think that I could."

Laughing softly, Pat replied, "No. We can clean up later. I don't think my legs will hold me up."

Sue giggled along with him. "Thank you for the meal," she groaned. "Although it may be my last. I don't think I'll live through the night.

Pat laughed out loud.

"Oh, don't say that," he replied, "I have something planned for us this Friday when we both have off."

"Really?" she said, now sitting up and clearly interested. "What, pray tell, kind of mess have you gotten us into this time, Stanley?" she asked, referring to Laurel and Hardy who were favorites of both of them.

Scratching the top of his head with a goofy smile, he said, "Well, Ollie, I thought that we would drive up to Penn's Falls outside of Ranksberg and rent a canoe from this place I know of. We can take it down the Oranoak River to Suskill. And we can stop along the way and have a picnic lunch on the shore."

"What about our car?"

"They will drive it down to Suskill for us and pick up the boat. It is their dock that we go to in Suskill."

"That sounds like fun. How long of a trip is it?"

Pat tilted his head and pursed his lips as he thought. "I'd say no more than five hours, tops. It's about twenty-five miles of river, but the Oranoak has a very swift current for a river. Especially upriver near its source in the mountains. It will make the paddling so much easier. I'll steer."

"Oh, sure," Sue laughed, "the man always wants to drive."

"You never use your signals when you drive," Pat protested.

"What are you talking about?" she laughed. "I always use my signals. Besides, we're in a boat. What signals?"

Pat was rolling with laughter. Sue started also.

"I like the idea, Pat," she said after their laughter subsided. "We should get up there early."

"Okay, I'll pick you up at eight o'clock in the morning. Cool?"

"Perfect."

§   §   §

On Thursday, Ted pulled the Gator into the parking space near the "log cabin" ranger station. It was a beautiful October day. The weather had been warm for the end of October. Unusually so. Ted smiled, thinking that the youngsters will have a good time this Halloween, knowing they won't have to wear a lot of constricting warm clothes under their costumes.

So far, the four rangers had been able to manage the shifts with one man down. Tony Wells wouldn't be back until mid- November. Almost every state park in the United States remained open all year long. At Shawtuck there really wasn't much to offer during the winter months. A large hill near the entrance to the park was used, in the winter (when there was snow) for sledding, tobogganing and snowboarding. That was about it for general recreation.

Because there were hardly any people using the park, except for the hill, in the winter months, hunters and trappers were allowed to hunt according to the state hunting laws. The park rangers mostly just checked hunting licenses and made sure they were using the correct firearms and only hunted the seasonally approved game. Over the years, fortunately, there had been very few hunting accidents in Shawtuck. There was a campground that the hunters were allowed to use for up to three days while they hunted. Every so often the rangers would have to go up there and reign in drunken campers. But there were never any big problems. They were a respectful bunch.

Entering the ranger station, Ted saw Sue pouring herself a cup of coffee.

"Hey, boss," she said, turning to look at him. "Everything go alright?"

"Yeah," he replied, "just a twisted ankle. The dad had taken his son for his first time hunting and the kid insisted on wearing tennis sneakers.

"Sneakers?" Sue exclaimed. "The father let him?"

Ted shrugged, good-naturally, "Seems so. I don't think he'll do that again." Sue snickered. "What, if anything, do you have planned for your day off tomorrow?" Ted asked.

Sue brightened up with a big smile.

"Oh, Pat is going to pick me up early and we're going to go canoeing."

"Great," Ted responded, going for a cup of coffee himself. "Sounds like fun. So, how is it going with Officer Patrick? He seems like a nice guy."

"He is," she gushed. "I very much like him. We get along great and we really do think alike."

Sipping his hot brew, Ted said, "I'm glad you two found each other." He paused. "So where are you two going canoeing? Sunset Lake?"

"No, something a bit more challenging," she admitted. "We're renting a canoe in Penn's Falls and taking it down the Oranoak River to Suskill."

"Oh," he said, smile fading. "The current in that part of the river is pretty swift. At least until it widens out at Amberton before Suskill."

"Yes, I know," Sue said, "it should make it a little more challenging."

"Hmm," Ted grunted in acknowledgement. He took another sip of coffee.

"Listen, Susan," he said seriously, "can you do me a favor?" She looked at him quizzically. "A small favor."

"Sure," she answered.

"Will you take one of the small, mobile radios we have here? I'll be here tomorrow and will have one. Just in case you run into some trouble."

She glanced at him sideways with a small grin. "Trouble? What kind of trouble?" she snickered. "Sharks?"

Ted laughed, self-consciously.

Then she looked with knitted brows and asked him quietly, "You're not thinking about that school bus thing, are you? Those kids that people supposedly see sometimes? You're serious, aren't you?"

Ted shrugged nonchalantly, trying to appear unbothered.

"Those currents are strong. I just want you both to be all right in the river. That's all." He smiled at her.

She looked at him curiously.

"O-okay, Ted. If you want me to, then I'll take one before I leave today. I'll keep it in the canoe with us. Is that okay?"

He breathed a quiet sigh of relief.

"That's great, Sue. You guys should have a great time."

§   §   §

At the end of his shift, Ted clocked out and said goodnight to the next shift of rangers there. He walked to his truck and got inside. The sun was going down. He started up his vehicle and drove out of the entrance gate. Pausing on High River Road, he turned left and began his drive home. At a bend in the road, Ted came upon the site where, two years ago, the school bus had lost control and had broken through the guardrail and careened down the steep embankment to the rocks and the river below. The guardrail had since been replaced and reinforced. On a sudden whim, he pulled over to a shoulder on the opposite side of the road. He didn't know why, just a brief feeling.

Getting out of his truck, Ted crossed the road and looked down toward the river past the severed tree stump on the other side of the guardrail. Already, new branches were growing out of the scarred wood. The path down the embankment was filled with new growth and the large, thick tree near the bottom already had hidden its scars. He could see the large, flat rocks jutting out into the river. There, the gouges and deep scrapes in the stone were still evident. He was just about to turn and return to his truck when something on the rocks caught his eye. He squinted, but couldn't quite see what was lying in the middle of the largest stone.

Hesitating for a minute, Ted then stepped over the guardrail. Very carefully, he made his way down the ridge using saplings to control his descent. Finally, safely on the bottom, he made his way out onto the rocks; sometimes jumping from one to the other. The sky now was a brilliant orange. The setting sun made the purple clouds glow on the horizon.

As he walked out on the wide stone staring at the object lying out near the edge, he stopped.

At his feet was a book. It looked like it had been waterlogged. The cover was swollen and wet, although still readable. Ted looked around him. Nothing was within sight. Dropping his head down again, he stared at the book facing up at him.

The cover had colored drawings of a little boy and girl sitting beneath a leafy tree, smiling happily with little squirrels and rabbits gathered around them. The title of the book read ***A Child's Course in Nature Study.***

Eyes moist with tears, he started to shake. Ted knew exactly what the book was for, having seen them in the school children's hands a hundred times before.

Picking it up, he turned and started back to the shore. Hearing a splash, he whirled around. There was nobody there. Looking down at the rock, Ted turned and ran as fast as he could up the embankment to his car.

He knew those small wet footprints weren't there before.

§   §   §

The alarm rang at a quarter to seven in the morning. Sleepily, Sue reached over and turned it off. Stretching broadly, she felt her joints noisily snap into place. She lay there for a minute just relaxing, and then rolled over and jumped out of bed. Bare feet slapping on the floorboards, Sue walked into the bathroom to pee and then brush her teeth. Then, reaching over, she turned on the shower. Getting in, she washed herself down. As she rinsed her hair she sang an old Eagles tune.

Twenty minutes later, she dressed and then strolled into the kitchen for breakfast. She tuned the radio to her favorite station and had a large glass of orange juice. Then, after a bowl of cereal, toast and three cups of coffee it was a quarter to eight. One more bathroom trip and she stepped outside her apartment building. The warm sun was shining and she could hear the birds in the trees singing to each other. A good day to be alive.

Seven minutes later, Pat drove into her parking lot and pulled up in front of her. He stopped the car and got out.

"Ahoy, Captain Ahab," he called out, "are we off to catch the white whale?"

Laughing, Sue said loudly, "Better that movie, than taking the canoe trip in "Deliverance".

Pat made a pained face and grabbed the seat of his jeans. "Ouch! Don't even say that in jest. That was horrible."

She laughed and walked up to him. They had a long kiss, said hello, and then got into his car.

"I have a picnic basket in the backseat filled with goodies and a great bottle of Poulet Montrachet. Went for my lungs, but it will be worth it."

"Oooo," she gushed, "Fancy Dan."

"Only the best for my first mate," he said as they sat down in the front seats.

"Wait," she said, giggling, "I thought I was Captain Ahab. When did I get the demotion?" He laughed.

They pulled away and drove out of the apartment complex. Soon they were on the road north. As they rode on, they eventually wound up parallel to the Oranoak River which went in and out of view as they drove on. The autumn colors were in full bloom. There were fewer and fewer houses and businesses as they drove on. As they rode, they casually talked about nature and about their likes and dislikes. Ice cream-yes, hot dogs-no, action movies-yes, foreign movies-a definite no. They disagreed on books, with her loving to read and him not reading a book unless his life depended on it.

"Jeez, I just don't understand it," she said, a bit surprised. "Reading is like taking a magical trip somewhere. You can get lost in a book."

"My only problem with reading," Pat said, "is that there are all of these words put together. And then you have to remember what they said when you close the book. I'll wait for the movie."

Sue pushed his arm.

"The movie is never as good as the book, Pat."

"You're wrong," he replied, "I always find the movie is much better."

She stared at him in surprise. "Really? You like the movies better?"

"Sure," he said to her, turning with a mischievous grin. "That's because I don't read the book."

"Ugh," she spat in feigned disgust. "You're impossible. A barbarian."

A few more miles up and Pat turned off the road. He drove up to a long, low, green building that had a sign reading **Bill's Bait and Tackle and Canoe Rentals**. Three trucks were parked in front.

They got out and walked into the store. It was filled with fishing rods, reels, creels, flies, outdoor clothes and hip boots. Behind the counter stood Bill. He was a tall man with wide shoulders, and a salt and pepper beard. What little hair that was on his head he had tied behind him in an embarrassingly sparse ponytail.

"Hey, Pat," he said as they walked up, "gonna do a little fishing today?"

"Not this time, Bill," he answered. "We're here to rent one of your canoes and take a trip down to Suskill on the Oranoak."

Bill smiled. He had more spaces than pearly whites.

"Oh, taking the scenic tour, are you? Bring a picnic basket?"

"Sure did. It's in the car."

"Let me get Neil to pick out a canoe for you. He'll take your keys and meet you down in Suskill. Two oars?"

Pat nodded. Bill winked at Sue.

"He's got you manning the galley, eh?" Bill threw his head back and laughed hardily.

Pat took care of the paperwork and payment and then they walked outside and down to a long dock. He had retrieved the picnic basket from the car and they walked out to a middle-aged man in a beat-up pair of jeans, boat shoes and an olive green thermal undershirt. His hair was in dire need of a combing and his face in need of a shave. As they reached him, he and Pat shook hands. Pat handed him his car keys. Then, the man gave them a short, perfunctory briefing on canoe safety.

"Don't worry, Pat. I'll be waiting for you in Suskill. Have a safe trip and, again, mind the currents. They can get a bit arduous."

Pat smiled and said, "Thanks, Neil. Will do."

As the man walked away, Sue watched him go. She turned to Pat and whispered, "Arduous? Ah, really?"

Pat glanced at the retreating figure. "Speaking of reading, you can't judge a book by its cover. Neil, there, used to teach abstract math and string theory at Yale before just walking away one day, coming back to his home and doing this. He said he had had it with academia and the ivory towers."

"Wow," Sue said in awe.

"You can never tell."

"I'll say," she agreed.

Pat held the canoe for Sue as she stepped into it. He then handed her the basket after she sat. Then he stepped in and sat on the seat. They took the oars and Pat pushed them away from the dock.

They rowed toward the center of the river as they began to feel the underwater currents take ahold and begin to carry the canoe forward. Sue reached into her purse and pulled out the radio connecting them to the Shawtuck ranger station. She set it in the picnic basket.

§   §   §

When Ted arrived in the park preserve he went to his desk and sat down. He placed the book he had picked up on the rocks yesterday on his desk. There, he stared at it with trepidation. To him this was some sort of dire omen of horror to come. He had finally admitted to himself that he was scared. He didn't hear Evan enter.

"Geez, where did you find that?" he said standing behind Ted.

The head ranger jumped in his seat and spun his head around.

"Hey, I didn't mean to scare you, boss. I haven't seen one of those books for a while," Evan continued. He reached down and touched the damp book with his finger.

"What, did you find this up in the woods? Some kid must have dropped it a long while ago." As he pressed his finger on the book, a rivulet of water ran out.

Wrinkling his nose, Evan remarked, "Eww, you should get rid of that. It smells terrible. Like something died in there." He chuffed, and then walked away.

Ted stared down at the book again, watching the thin finger of water work its way down his desk toward him.

Like something died in there.

Ted grabbed the book by the edge and then threw into the waste basket alongside his desk. Then quickly wiped his hand on his trousers.

§   §   §

The sun shone in the autumn sky as the canoe continued down the river.

"Boy," Sue called back to Pat, "you almost don't even have to paddle much. The current does most of the work for you."

"Yeah," he called from the rear, "that's the beauty of the Oranoak River. The currents do all of the work. This works until you go all the way down to Amberton. Then, the river starts to widen and the current loses its strength on the silty bottom. By the time you reach Suskill, the current is weak. There it's almost as wide as a small lake. A lot of underwater plants clog up the sides."

Sue looked at her watch.

"We are almost at the three hour mark. The trees and foliage have been breathtaking. Did you see that group deer drinking at the water's edge?"

"I did," Pat remarked. "Very cool. Are you getting hungry?"

"Just about there, Pat."

"Good. I was thinking of stopping a little before the park entrance. There is a small clearing off to the right, with the jetty of sand. It would be an easy stop."

"I would have thought this series of long, flat rocks that jut out nearer the park."

"Nah," Pat said. "All those underwater rocks near the shore are dangerous to try to navigate."

"Works for me then, Pat," Sue said looking back at him.

§   §   §

Miles downriver in the town of Suskill, a series of mechanical dredging machines had begun to be offloaded, along the side of the Oranoak River. The state of Pennsylvania had finally approved Suskill Township's request to build a recreational marina along the banks of the river. The actual building of the marina was to begin in the spring, but the town fathers wanted to take advantage of the good weather to begin the basic dredging of the shoreline. They wanted to even out and widen the area. There was a hook in the river between Amberton and Suskill that they wanted eliminated. It was a snarl of underwater roots, marshes and silt buildup. All of that needed to be removed. They had hoped to quickly get that done before winter. The actual marina was going to be a complicated project and they wanted to get a head start and get an idea what they had to work with. It was already the day before Halloween and the engineers figured they had at most, two more weeks, maybe three, to finish the dredging.

§   §   §

Evan ran into the station.

"Ted, a trapper out by Killian's Creek just got his hand caught in a trap."

"Start the Gator, I'll call EMS."

Ted spoke quickly on the phone and then slamming it down, ran out the door and jumped into the Gator with Evan. The two rangers took off into the forest.

The radio connected to Sue sat on the corner of his desk, forgotten.

§   §   §

After pulling into the shallows, they beached the canoe. Getting out, Sue and Pat brought out the picnic basket and carried it to the shore. Pat had a large tartan plaid blanket over his shoulder.

Walking off the U-shaped, sandy beach, they spread the blanket in a quiet, grassy area. They sat down on the wool blanket and opened the large basket. To Susan's pleasant surprise, the basket contained plates, silverware, wineglasses, a mélange of various cheeses, meats, fruits and a long French bread. Pat uncorked the bottle of wine.

They spread everything out and then Pat poured the glasses of wine for them.

"To us," he said with a warm smile.

Returning his smile and clinking glasses, Sue said the same. Birds were in the trees singing and they could hear the insects buzzing. The river bubbled pleasantly past them. Everything was perfect.

They made little sandwiches with the bread; each one containing a different combination of meats and cheeses. They had a small bunch of grapes that they fed to each other, while laughing and sipping wine. It was so quiet and lovely. Soon, the hand-feeding of grapes started to turn sensual with increasing kissing involved.

Sue looked around coyly and asked, "Can anyone see us here?"

"Of course not," Pat said softly, "we are hidden from the road. Not that anyone travels it much."

Smiling, she pulled him down and they immediately began kissing passionately and pulling on each other's clothes. Soon they were naked and making fevered love.

§   §   §

Ted and Evan guided the groaning trapper to the Gator. They carefully sat him down.

"Don't touch the trap, Fred. Leave it alone."

"Jesus," he moaned, "but it hurts so freaking bad. Christ!"

"It will be okay, Fred," Ted said. "Right now it's the only thing holding your fingers together. Let's keep it there until the doctors see it. Okay?"

The twenty-eight-year-old man nodded with a teary grimace. "Yeah, yeah, okay. Fuck."

They drove back down to the office. Already, Ted could hear the distant wailing of the ambulance coming. *Another day as a forest ranger,* Ted thought.

§   §   §

Sue and Pat were just getting dressed when they heard the siren of an ambulance go speeding down the road.

Sue quickly turned to Pat and said, trying her best not to laugh, "Pat, are you okay? You didn't break anything did you?"

The both burst into laughter, hugging each other and kissing. Holding each other closely on the blanket, half dressed, they both were suddenly overwhelmed by how absolutely perfect everything was.

Eventually, they sat up, dressed and started to put the picnic basket back together again.

As they were placing things back into their spots, Pat looked over at Sue and stopped for a second. "You know that I am falling in love with you."

She sat back, grinning warmly. "Yes, I do." She gazed into his eyes. "And I'm in love with you, too. I feel so lucky."

§　　　　　　§　　　　　　§

Steve Murray sat watching the game on television in his easy chair. He had just finished his second beer.

"Steve," his wife called from the kitchen. "Steve, Goldie has to go out." There was a brief pause. "Steve!" she called out again. "Did you hear me? Goldie has to go out. Now."

"Yeah, yeah, Iris, I heard you. I'm not deaf, you know. I can hear."

"Well, sometimes I can't tell if you can't hear me or you're just being stubborn and ignoring me."

"Oh, brother," he mumbled to himself. "Fifty-five years of marriage. Death where is thy sting?"

"What did you say?" Iris called out again. "I can't hear you. You mumble all the time. What have I always told you about speaking up so a person can hear you? Time and time again☐"

"Okay, okay, Iris, I'm getting up."

The seventy-eight-year-old retired tool and die maker pushed himself up. Grunting with exertion, he called out,

"Goldie! Come on! Time to go out."

The ten year old golden retriever came bounding in from the kitchen, tongue lolling out of her smiling, open mouth.

"Okay girl," Steve said, as she jumped up on him with excitement. "Let's go find your leash."

§   §   §

Back in the canoe again, Pat pushed them out and they turned and continued down the Oranoak River. They were just letting the current take them. They both really didn't want to trip to end too soon.

§   §   §

The EMS workers closed the ambulance doors and ran around to the front cab. Getting in they slammed the doors shut and sped out of the lot heading to Suskill and South Shawtuck Hospital. Carol came up and said, "All good?"

"Hopefully," Evan said. "They may have to reattach two or three fingers."

"Maybe two," Ted replied. "One was just badly cut."

"What happened?" Carol asked.

"George of the Jungle there, stuck his hand into his own trap retrieving it," Ted chuckled. Turning to Evan, Ted asked him, "Did you take a lunch break, yet?"

"Not yet," Evan said. "Lost my appetite there."

Ted smiled slightly.

"Okay, I'll take fifteen minutes and grab a bite."

Evan went inside to take care of the paperwork. Carol took one of the Gators to take a look at the hill used for sledding in the winter. She wanted to see what new growth needed to be removed before the winter activities began.

Ted went inside and into the kitchen area they had for the staff. He took two cheese, bacon, and tomato on rye sandwiches he had brought and put them into the toaster oven.

The radio, still temporarily forgotten, sat out on his desk.

§ § §

Goldie pulled Steve Murray down the street, stopping at every other tree. None seem to be the one to receive the anointing of her urine.

They wound up at the end of the street where it met High River Road. Knowing what was eventually coming; Steve groaned and let Goldie guide him across the street and over the rail. It was the same thing almost every time. Steve shook his head. She was getting too old for these gymnastics and he, for sure, was.

§   §   §

The canoe began to pick up a little speed. They both could see the increasing amount of rocks and boulders begin to accumulate along the bank and into the river itself. Sue knew vaguely that that was the eventual result of the farthest extension of the prehistoric Ice Age glaciers in this area of America. The boulders had been carried miles and miles by the ever-expanding glacial edge, and then left here when the ice retreated.

"I'll guide us through the rocks," Pat called out. "Let me know if you see something in front of us. This shouldn't be too bad."

Sue could see, down the river, the jutting projection of the collection of large, flat rocks that stuck out into the river. She knew this was where the bus accident occurred. But they weren't really near the rocks on the shore side.

As they glided forward and could hear the water gurgling around the protruding stones. The canoe seemed to veer toward the side and then abruptly turned. Suddenly, the canoe slammed to a stop. Both Sue and Pat were thrown to the bottom of the boat.

"What happened?" Pat shouted out.

Sue grabbed the front of the canoe and pulled herself forward.

"We're stuck on something," she called back. "Let me see what it is." Sue leaned over and looked into the clear, rushing waters.

"Oh, shit," she yelled, pulling back.

"What," Pat called out. "What is it?"

"It…it looks like the partial grille of some vehicle. I think it's a bus. It's yellow."

§   §   §

Goldie dragged Steve down along the shoreline. Here in Amberton, the embankment was not steep at all. The biggest impediment on this part of the river was the tangle of bushes and plant life along the shore. For years it was all too tangled and impossible to walk through. But the dredging that had already started here had made the shoreline much more accessible to anyone who wanted to walk down here. Not that anyone really wanted to. The fact the river bent around this point created a little pool in this area. The water, trapped here, became stagnant and smelled to high heaven with rotting vegetation. The excess silt became like quicksand along the shore.

The new dredging had cleared out much of the floral growth and had removed the sand bars that had built up over the years and helped create the swamp-like snag.

Steve was able to walk along the shoreline freely for the first time that he could ever remember. Goldie seemed absolutely adamant to continue her path down the shoreline, sniffing everything as if it were perfume.

§   §   §

"A bus grille?" Pat said, surprised.

Just then, as he sat there stunned and Sue was gazing over the side at the twisted metal grille, a small hand emerged from the water and grabbed the side of the canoe.

"Oh, shit," Pat screamed.

As Sue looked behind her, two more hands reached up and grabbed each side of the boat.

"Oh, my God," she screamed. "Oh, my God."

Two heads broke the surface of the water. They were the long dead faces of little children.

"Oh God, it's true," Sue whispered.

She dove to the center of the boat and grabbed the radio now lying on the bottom. Hitting the button, she called.

"Ted, Ted, it's Sue. Answer me."

§　　　　　　§　　　　　　§

Ted was just about to start on his second sandwich when the radio on his desk squawked. He jumped up and ran out to his desk, wiping his mouth roughly with a napkin. Grabbing the radio, he hit the button and answered.

"Sue, it's Ted. What's wrong?"

§　　　　　　§　　　　　　§

"We're in the river by the rocks. Where the bus crashed. There are things in the water attacking the canoe. They're kids. Dead kids. They're trying to tip us over."

More hands had emerged and kept shaking the boat. Pat was batting the hands with his oar.

"Come play with us," they called eerily. "We've been waiting for you. We're so cold and lonely."

"Jesus, Ted," Sue shrieked, "can you hear that?"

He could. God save him, he could hear those eerie voices.

The boat swung over to the side, nearer the jutting, flat rocks. She clung to the front of the canoe not wanting to be flung into the river.

A small, white face, immediately below the surface smiled up at Sue. It was little girl and she gestured for her to jump into the water with her.

§   §   §

"I'm on my way there," Ted yelled over the radio. "I'm coming."

Ted jumped up from the chair and ran out the door to his truck. He started it and abruptly spun around in a cloud of leaves and dust, and tore out of the entrance. Making a screeching turn left, he sped down High River Road, cutting off an oncoming car. A first.

§   §   §

Steve stumbled over a thick vine and almost went down to his knees.

"For the love of God, Goldie," he growled, "What's gotten into you?"

His golden retriever was tugging relentlessly at her leash. She was growling now.

"Slow down, I can't keep up." He tried tugging her back, to no avail.

§   §   §

"Jump onto the rocks, Sue!" Pat shouted out. The canoe shifted closer. "Jump."

"What about you?" she replied.

"I'll be right behind you," he yelled. "Just go."

The pale hands were tugging at the sides of the canoe harder and harder.

"Join us." the ghostly voices called.

Then, just as the canoe tilted toward the rocks, Sue stepped on the seat and jumped for her life. She hit the water only three feet from the largest rock. The icy water shocked her. She started swimming and splashing toward it frantically.

§   §   §

Ted's truck skidded to a halt in the road and he jumped out. Quickly vaulting the guardrail, he saw the canoe out in the river and Pat slamming the oar at the hands grabbing the sides.

Taking a controlled tumble down the steep embankment, he popped up and ran out onto the rocks on the river, jumping from one to another.

Sue had reached the rock and grabbed the flat surface. She started to pull herself up when a hand grabbed her ankle. As hard as she struggled to pull herself up, the hand tugged her steadily back down into the rushing waters. The surface of the flat rock was becoming slippery from the water and her sweat. She slowly began to lose her tenuous grip. Just then, Ted reached her and with a mighty tug, pulled her out of the river.

She lay on the stone, gasping and sputtering.

The canoe rocked back and forth violently, as Pat struggled to remain standing. As it finally seemed ready to tip over, Pat desperately vaulted himself out. He stretched his body out, lunging for the rocks. But the boat had turned again, and with a big splash he landed in the river seven feet from the jutting rock.

Ted laid himself down on his stomach on the flat stone and stretching out, reached out for the furiously struggling young cop.

"Give me your hand, Pat. Reach out for me."

§   §   §

Goldie stopped short and started barking furiously at the fetid water in front of her.

"There's nothing out there, girl. Stop that," Steve pleaded. He was exhausted.

He placed himself in front of her to try and get his dog to turn away; but she was singularly focused on the water in front of her. The dredging hours earlier had muddied up the river water here.

Panting and trying to catch his wind, Steve stood erect to take a deep breath.

Just then, Goldie lunged forward, barking even louder. Her sudden momentum hit him and made Steve stumble back. His feet slid off of the wet grass on the shore, and he fell back into the waist deep water. He flailed helplessly, kicking and waving his arms as he struggled in the water trying to stand.

Pat was a good swimmer and as he began to paddle toward Ted, against the pulling currents, several hands grabbed him from below. They tugged and yanked on his body and clothes as he fought against the currents. A young boy emerged from the water and grabbed him. Stroking the water with adrenaline surged strength, Pat swam with all of his might.

Ted leaned over the edge of the rock as far as he dared. As he did, a little girl's face appeared from beneath the water. Her sunken and rotten face was hideous. As his eyes widened with fright, she smiled at him.

"Come with me," he heard in his head.

Coughing and choking, Steve spit the foul river water from his mouth. Goldie was barking even louder, her eyes almost bulging out of her head. She was jumping and running around as if crazed. She looked as if she was trying to jump in after him but was too afraid to.

"Okay, Goldie, I'm all right. Jesus."

Reaching out from the water to pet her and calm her down, Steve saw a piece of sodden cloth wrapped around his arm. As he pulled the fabric from his arm he could see that it looked like an old, ripped piece of children's clothing. Looking around in the murky water surrounding him, there suddenly were bodies that came floating up to the surface. Not one or two, but many bloated bodies, all children, that were shaken loose from the muck and roots that had held them down there for two years.

Eyes bulging out, Steve started gagging and then screaming at the top of his lungs in sheer and unbridled terror.

A passing police patrol car heard his horrified, blood-curdling screams and stopped. The two officers ran over to the guardrail and looked over.

They froze in disbelief.

Suddenly, like ropes being freed, the hands slipped off of Pat and he paddled over and grabbed onto Ted's outstretched hand. The ranger pulled him up out of the river. He lay there next to Sue gasping and choking. They grabbed each other and wouldn't let go.

Ted sat there staring out into the Oranoak River. The overturned canoe was pulled loose by the current and continued to float swiftly down the dark river to its final destination.

An ambulance was called and Sue Cummings and Pat Kaiser were taken to the hospital. They were quickly released with no injuries, save for a few minor scratches.

Steve Murray was also taken to the hospital, where he was admitted with a sudden heart attack. He also developed a nasty bacterial infection from ingesting the contaminated river water. After a couple of weeks of medication, he eventually recovered and returned home to his wife's care. He wanted to stay in longer. He never walked Goldie along the shoreline again.

High River Road was soon clogged with police cars from Amberton, Mercerville and Mayors Landing. A number of ambulances came and went with their sad cargo of drowned bodies. The county medical examiner determined all of their deaths were from drowning. As far as any other suspicious marks, well, they were submerged for too long to determine anything.

By the end of the medical examination and the multi-jurisdictional police inquiry, the dozen bodies that were discovered after a thorough and long search were determined by the Army Corps of Engineers to have been all guided there by the river currents and the shape and natural composition of the shoreline. They were surprised that the bodies traveled that far (although there was a class action law suit eventually brought against the original police search.

No adult bodies of the several missing adults were ever found.

The recovered bodies found included:

Sophia Allman

Robert McCord

Samantha Riesling } all from Mayors Landing

Jeffrey Williams

Lauren Meyerson

□□ □□

James Freeman

David Ballantine

Richard Carlton

Kenneth Sims } all from Mercerville

Gary Springer

Michael LoPresti

Andrew Kozak

§   §   §

The winter came and went without another incident along High River Road. The spring and summer also had nothing untoward happen. Apparently, whatever hauntings or sightings had ended with the finding and removal of the bodies.

This, of course, didn't stop the urban legends that had sprung up around all of the unexplained happenings in the area. But after a while the curious "ghost hunters" began to lose interest and the area returned to normal.

But that situation, combined with what had happened in the New York State portion of the Shawtuck State Forest Preserve and the old, abandoned insane asylum there, unfortunately gave the Shawtuck Mountains an evil and supernatural reputation that was to last for a long, long time.

But, the asylum story is for another time and another book.

The End

Author

Richard McCrohan has been interested in the supernatural and uncanny for as long as he could remember. He enjoys the emotional rollercoaster that a good, scary book will bring its reader. That creepy feeling you get while reading that makes you rise from your easy chair and turn on all the lights in your room (especially that dark hallway that you just heard a noise in).

The Children in the River marks Mr. McCrohan's nineteenth book published to date. It proudly joins his brood of literary offspring meant to titillate your imagination and send a chill up your spine.

Richard McCrohan lives in Boynton Beach, Florida and can be reached at Rjjmac51@comcast.net.

Richard McCrohan,

October, 2024

Made in the USA
Columbia, SC
06 September 2024

4d9ee3c2-d8a8-44e5-ad65-e32f2e6217dcR01